For John Huddleston, who liked to believe in fairies!

Gateway Stone Spectacles

With the lenses removed and
devil eyes put in their place

THE MYSTERY OF THE
FOOL & THE VANISHER

Being an investigation into the life and disappearence of Isaac Wilde, artist and fairy seeker

David and Ruth Ellwand

CANDLEWICK PRESS
CAMBRIDGE, MASSACHUSETTS

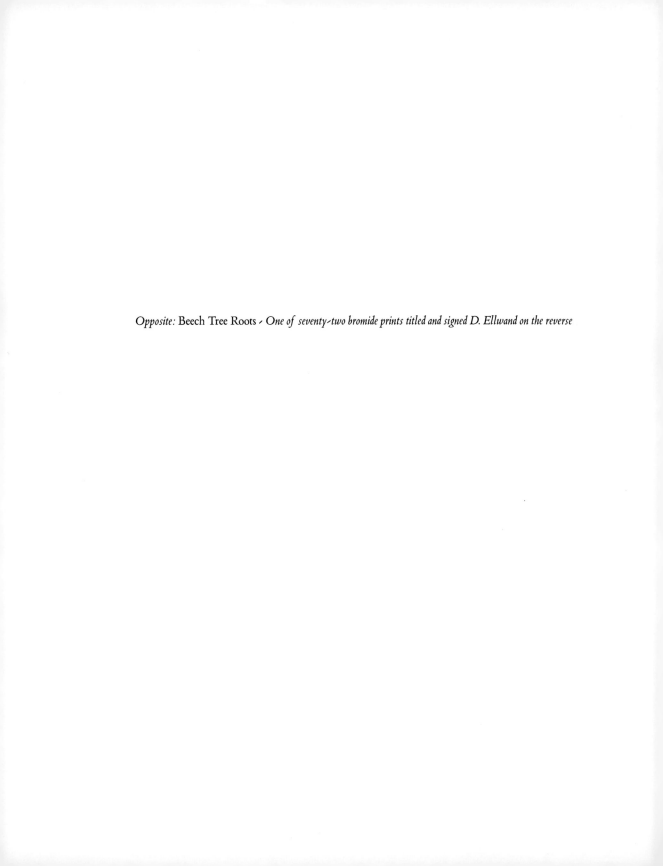

Opposite: Beech Tree Roots ⁄ *One of seventy-two bromide prints titled and signed D. Ellwand on the reverse*

PART ONE

David Ellwand's personal journal with additional notes from his photographic notebook

Honour is the key; never take what is not yours. ~ Re Et Merito

I walk on the Downs in the footsteps of Conan Doyle and Kipling. It's a beautiful place, full of mystery and magic. Any time of year, there is something to see, whether you walk past the dying poppies of late summer or crack the frozen puddles of winter.

The South Downs have always been special: Neolithic man was the first to harvest their bounty of flint stone, digging deep to find the best veins in order to fashion fine tools and, of course, start fire. All ages of man since have walked the Downs. The ground is etched with the remains of hill forts and tumuli (ancient burial mounds)—even the Romans trod the gentle, rolling slopes. Today, if you are lucky, you might still find a finely worked flint arrowhead there.

A Path on the Downs

I know of a special place here, a hill, and, if local legends are to be believed, a haunted hill. Apparently at dusk you can see some type of evil fairy. I'd like to believe it would still be possible to see such a thing, but these days there's a scientific explanation for everything.

I think I should at this point explain my understanding of what a "fairy" or "faery" is. Customs and folklore tell us that they are small ethereal beings. The "fae," as they are often known, include pixies, goblins, elves (both dark and light), brownies, grims, will-o'-the-wisps, and sprites. All of these so-called creatures are the same—it's just different interpretations at different times by different human beings that lead to the confusion of titles. I myself believe they are a disenfranchised group of feral pygmies that inhabit the inner earth, living in caves and mines that they leave only when no human is around.

Looking South to Barrow Hill

Untitled

In the gentle lowlands of the Downs grow ancient woodlands stunted and bent from the sea wind that howls along the valleys and breaks upon the trees. If you walk straight over the haunted hill and down into the vale, you come to my favorite wood. Here, every tree has a story to tell. You can imagine, if spirits are anywhere, this is where they'd be, darting in and out of the holes in the tree trunks and fighting among the tangled roots. It's a beautiful and serene place, but it's also dark, eerie, and dead scary.

And here my story began—when I found a stone.

Above: Lightning Tree

FINDERS KEEPERS

My stone is perfect. As old as time, made of gray flint, and the size of a walnut, it has a large hole straight through it. Since the moment I picked it out from among the worn and tangled roots, it has stayed with me. I wear it around my neck on a silver chain.

In folklore the holed stone plays an important role. Known as a hagstone, witch stone, flint ring, gateway stone, faerie stone, pix stone, or devil eye, such a talisman is said to protect you from evil, especially the spells of witches. It is even said to let you see the fae if you look through the hole. The stone can also protect you from nightmares—just hang it on your bedpost or place it under your pillow.

I have read many stories about such stones. The stone must always be flint—the rock of sparks— and the hole must be naturally worn by the elements. Never try to make one yourself. It won't work! A good stone, if carried at all times, will bring luck; whether the luck is good or bad depends on the holder. Never try to find a special stone; if you are meant to own one, it will find you. Never string the stones together—if they touch one another, they lose their power. If the stone comes into contact with metal, its power increases.

It used to be that every day I'd look through my stone in the hope of seeing something mystical, but I'd never see anything . . .

Above: Holed Flint Stone ⌐
Found among the beech tree roots

Right: Beech Tree Roots

until that one day, in the woods. It was a miserable January late afternoon, dark, dank. I looked through the hole in my stone, and, lo and behold, I saw a light dart between the trees. When I took the stone away from my eye, I saw nothing.

35-mm Contact Sheet - *Ilford FP4 plus film*

{15}

Again I looked through the stone, and there it was! The ball of light swooped down through the branches and hovered in front of my face, then shot forward at an unbelievable speed.

Quickly, I followed, but it was too fast.

I ran past the gnarled trees and found myself in a clearing. There stood an old, dilapidated house. It had been empty for many years. The sense of desolation was overwhelming—I had to go inside. I went through the doorway and looked around at the faded patterns of worn wallpaper, rusting gas mantles hanging from ceilings, a table buckling under the weight of rubble from the fallen roof. I didn't know what had happened here, but obviously someone had left in a hurry.

I came out, looked at the teetering chimney pot, took some photographs, and walked around the back, and that's when I found it, in the old outhouse — a wooden chest.

Left: Footpath to the Abandoned House   *Following pages:* The Former Lodgings of Isaac Wilde

The chest had obviously been there a very long time. It was covered in dirt and cobwebs, and the padlock and chain around it were rusted solid. I cleared the broken pots and bits of rubbish from the top and tried to force the lock, but it was impossible. I grabbed the handles on the side of the chest and tried lifting it. Although it was very heavy, I did manage to slide it off the shelf and let it drop to the ground. I realized that the chest must have been packed full of something, and I knew I had to have it. I did something I shouldn't have done. Leaving a harrow in the ground, I dragged the chest out onto the old footpath. Home was three miles away, much too far to manage, so I simply hid the chest amongst the bracken and returned to the studio.

There are places you should not go, and inside that chest was one of those places.

The Chest in the Outhouse

The Chest - *2 feet x 2 feet;
secured with a lock and chain*

How was I ever going to get the chest home? After studying a map, I decided the only way was to drag the box through the woods. The next day, I set off before daybreak with a piece of rope. When I arrived at the house, I located the chest, tied the ends of my rope to the handles at either side, and started pulling. Two hours later I had managed to get the chest to my car. With great difficulty I hauled it into the back, and then I drove to my studio. Once there, I couldn't wait any longer. With a crowbar, I pried the lock open, breaking the hasp, and slowly lifted the lid.

The Chest Opened —

Photographed as found

RELICS & REMAINS

When the lid opened, the sweet smell of age, like an old library, was the first thing I noticed. I know I should have made efforts to inform the authorities—after all, this might be considered a treasure trove—but, hey, finders keepers. As far I was concerned, it was mine. Slowly I unpacked the chest, taking care not to damage any of the items. There was so much to discover, layer after layer, and the more I delved, the more I became obsessed, as if taken over by a power from within the box.

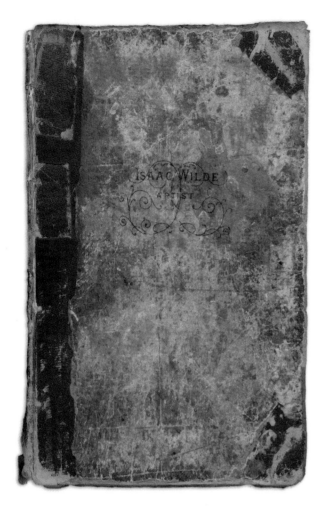

Above: The Cover of Isaac Wilde's Journal ⁃ *Cardboard with leather binding, Octavo*

Above right: Journal Page ⁃ *Seeds applied to paper*

Far right: Journal Pages ⁃ *Sketches by Isaac Wilde with pressed pansy flowers*

The chest belonged to a Mr. Isaac Wilde—at least, that was the name printed on one of the journals within. The books contained very few words, so I found it very difficult to grasp the content.

Inside the chest was a smaller wooden box, and inside this were three cardboard containers.

I carefully removed the top of one of these tubes and found a cylindrical object covered in mold. At first I had no clue what it was, but after a little research, I discovered it was a wax phonograph sound recording. I contacted a specialist who told me it might be possible to still hear what was recorded on the cylinder. He offered to try playing it on one of his antique phonograph machines. I sent the wax cylinders to him, and four weeks later a CD arrived.

Nothing could have prepared me for what I heard when I listened to the disk. There behind a loud crackle was the voice of Mr. Wilde, and he had a very strange story to tell indeed.

Using the contents of the chest

and a transcript of the wax recording,

I now present the strange case of

the fool and the vanisher.

Phonograph Cylinder - 4½ x 2½ inches,

wax, with cardboard cover

PART TWO

Being a complete transcript of the phonograph recordings of Isaac Wilde

documented here alongside photographs of the contents of the wooden box

Mask: Carte de Visite
[previous page]
Gold-toned albumen print
mounted on card
2½ x 4 inches

Friday, *Jan. 18, 1889*

I have just taken delivery of this wonderful new

phonograph voice-recording machine acquired from

a friend in exchange for some old cameras.

This evening I attended a dinner held in my honor by the London

Photographic Society, which has seen fit to recognize my artistic work

by the award of certain medals. I was pleased to attend, since the artistic

merits of the photographic function in these modern times are rarely

acknowledged—and are, indeed, in some quarters,

fiercely contested. After dinner, my friend Henry,

Two Photography Prize Medals
*1. West London
Photographic Society*
Bronze, 1½ inches,
1.69 ounces
2. First prize medal
Gilt bronze, 1¾ inches,
1.34 ounces

Gibson Gayle

Portrait of Gibson Gayle
*Gold-toned albumen
print mounted on card*
5 x 3¾ inches
Inscribed "Gibson Gayle"
in ink on the reverse

the Chairman of the Society, introduced me to a

certain Dr. Gibson Gayle, an interesting man and

member of the Sussex Archaeological Society. The

fellow displayed little knowledge of photography but was impressed by m

work and started, as scientists are wont to do, to quiz me about technique

and the like. Later, over a glass of fine claret, he told me about his plan to excavate a hill fort which he believed to have once been a Neolithic flint mine and which is rumored to be haunted. He expressed the wish that I join his team as Official Photographer. The dig is due to commence in the early spring, and his Society would cover all my expenses and even afford me a small stipend. Although having no real interest in archaeology, I am minded to accept the commission. My pecuniary circumstances do not permit me to refuse such an offer.

Wynne's Infallible Exposure Meter
Nickel-plated with enamel face

Friday, Feb. 15, 1889

Met with Gayle at his house to receive my instructions. Gayle, dismissive of the "pictorial" school of photography, held forth on art's sole purpose being the furtherance of science by the faithful transcription of objective reality. Through the spade, the camera, and his scribblings, Gayle proposes to conquer the ignorance of the masses, banishing all superstition.

33

Photographs by Isaac Wilde

View to Barrow Hill [main image]
Gold-toned albumen print
8½ x 5½ inches

Floral Still Life [top right]
Gold-toned albumen print
7 x 7 inches

Waterfall [bottom right]
Gold-toned albumen print
5 x 4 inches

FAI'RY (S.) an imaginary, little being, phantom, hobgoblin, or spirit, that the credulity of some, and the designs of others, have made to exist; pretending that they reward the industrious, and punish the lazy.

GNO'ME (S.) a name which the cabalists give to some certain invisible people, whom they suppose to inhabit the inner parts of the earth, and to fill it to the center; they are represented very small of stature, tractable, unfriendly to men, and are made the guardians of mines, quarries, hidden treasures, &c.

ELVES (S.) imaginary beings with which women frighten froward children, under the dreadful names of fairies, raw-head and bloody-bones, &c.

Monday, March 4, 1889

First day of Gayle's "dig." Most of the excavations are to be carried out by the members of the local Society, but today the farmworkers were put to heavy haulage and cartage. There was much talk amongst them of the "Pharisees" or fairies who are said to inhabit the hill and cause mischief, souring the milk on the hillside farms and replacing their children with "changelings" when enraged. Gayle has no time for such stories and took great delight in scaring the locals by reading out to them the definition of "FAIRY" inscribed in one of his learned books. I took the liberty of removing the definition afterwards and pasted it in my logbook. A sullen air fell over the activities on the hillside, and work proceeded in silence. I was intrigued by the local stories, however, and curious to find out more.

Quotations from an Early Book
Circa 1670 (unidentified)

Monday, March 18, 1889

I have spent these two weeks past photographing the local landscape and, on occasions, the dig. I have watched several hundred tons of chalk and flint being carted away, leaving open wounds in the hillside. I found many stones with holes through them. I obtained two coins and an ancient pottery flask from a farmworker in exchange for a photographic portrait of his girl. I may be able to earn myself a penny or two from these items.

I heard today from an old man farmer the strange tales of the pixies. The locals are afraid of the hill. They call the old flint mine Pixhole. And they firmly believe that the pixies steal their horses and cattle, apparently manifesting themselves in two ways. Children have reported seeing a tribe of pixies coming out of the mine. About nine inches tall, they wear some kind of battle dress while carrying tiny swords and shields. The children say that if you leave them alone,

Roman Coin [top left]

Copper
Diameter: 1 inch
Weight: 0.3 ounces

Inscribed "CAESAR AVG. IMP. M. OTHO." Marcus Salvius Otho was the emperor of Rome from January 15 to April 16, AD 69, the second emperor of the Year of the Four Emperors. Committed suicide after only three months. Very rare.

Roman Coin [top right]

Bronze
Diameter: 1⅛ inch
Weight: 0.4 ounces

Inscribed "IMP. CAESAR VESPASIANVS." Titus Flavius Vespasianus was emperor of Rome from 69 to 79. He is believed to have started the construction of the Colosseum.

Ampulla or Pilgrim's Flask from the Shrine of Saint Menas

Terra-cotta
3½ x 2½ inches

Byzantine; probably made at Abu Mena, near Alexandria, Egypt, between the fourth and seventh centuries. Ampullae were used by pilgrims to carry water or oil home from the great pilgrimage site for Saint Menas, said to be a late-third-century Egyptian Roman soldier who was martyred for his Christian faith. They have been discovered by archaeologists all over Europe.

they will not hurt you, but if you get in their way, you will become one

of them and join their tribe. No adult could recall seeing a pixie since

childhood. Another of the locals told me that the pixies are the keepers

of the stones and known as "black hats."

Photograph Album
12 x 8½ inches
Containing albumen and
gelatin-silver prints

Most of the local people prefer to believe the pixies

are ethereal beings, manifesting themselves as orbs of bright light. These orbs exit the mine on the hill at dusk and speed to the wood, where they hover till dawn. Every one of the locals, whether young or old, has seen the so-called "will-o'-the-wisp." Following the locals' directions, I have produced several artistic exposures of these beautiful ghostly phenomena.

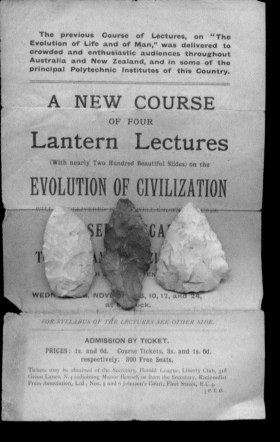

I have learned, too, that the sharp flints Gayle labels "arrowheads" are known by the locals as "pixshot" or "elfshot." Apparently these pixies are feisty little things, capable of doing great harm.

Because of these pervasive superstitions, the locals are not happy about disturbing the mine, and this morning several families left the hamlet near my lodging, vowing not to return until the archaeologists have gone.

All the locals wear holed stones strung around their necks, apparently to protect them from the evildoings of these pixies.

Three Neolithic Arrowheads
Knapped flint wrapped in an advertising flyer

Collodion-Positive Glass Plate
4 ¼ x 3 ¾ inches

The dig has so far uncovered the remains of an ancient hilltop fort, labeled by Gayle "Settlement," which, judging by the layer of carbonized turf that covers the postholes and bankings, once burned down and was never replaced. Gayle continues to delve farther, determined to uncover traces of earlier civilizations. He was warned by the local landowner not to disturb the roots of the ancient "King Oak" on the hill, but he saws through them, heedless. I recorded the measurements of the Great Oak and made a sketch for my own amusement.

Cir at A = 19.8
at 3'.6" from
ground

B.Cir = 8'-8"

C - = 23'-0"

D - = 46'-6"

Length of E from
trunk = 72.0

Dille of F = 63'-0 +
these are across
each other

-King of-
A-Oaks-

Friday, March 22, 1889

I feel I should note the events of today in all their peculiar detail, although they have left me agitated and scarcely able to concentrate. The morning was overcast and Gayle in a black rage. The workers, slipping and sliding as they carted the sodden spoil, were soundly berated by Gayle for their lack of speed. Grumbling, he descended into the trench. I found him scraping around in the dirt in the manner of a boar searching for truffles. At once, the scientist squealed and began to hop around. "Help me, Wilde—I've been shot!" he cried.

A small pin protruded from his fleshy calf. I removed the object, took out my pocket magnifier, and examined it closely. "There's your shot, Gayle," I said. "A sword—fashioned by the Little People themselves!"

"What nonsense you talk, Wilde. You know nothing whatsoever of the science of archaeology, and you pay too much heed to gossip. I am in pain and will certainly be lame from this." Cursing and muttering, Gayle made his way back to the surface. I wrapped the curious object in my kerchief and brought it back to my lodgings for safekeeping.

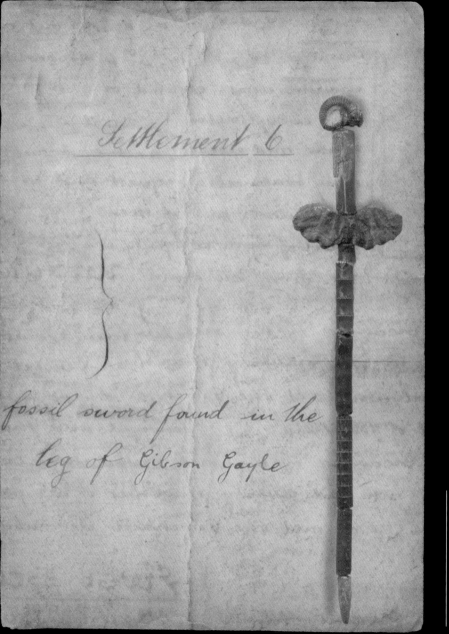

Settlement 6

fossil sword found in the
leg of Gibson Gayle

Sword
4½ inches
Small sword made of
fossils wrapped in a
sheet of paper with the
words "Settlement 6
fossil sword found in the
leg of Gibson Gayle"

Map Fragment
Showing Barrow Hill
5 ½ x 7 inches

The Workers
Two albumen prints
5 x 3¼ inches [below]
3 x 4 inches [right]
One gold-toned and mounted on card; both
inscribed "Workers" in pencil on the reverse

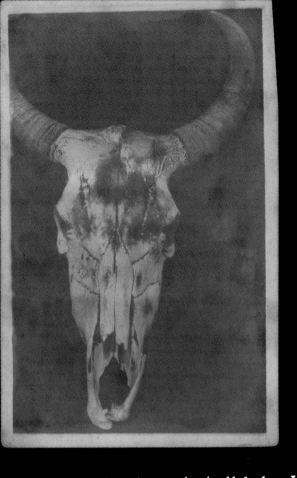

Skull
Gelatin-silver print
6½ x 4 inches
Mounted on card stamped
"Wilde Studios" on the reverse

Saturday, April 6, 1889

Today a shaft was uncovered some 21 feet down, leading to a large chamber. This was the Neolithic flint mine Gibson Gayle had been hoping to find. It didn't look like much to me, but from the hullabaloo I surmised that it must have been deemed very important to modern archaeology. Gayle contacted senior members of his Society, who duly met on the hill. They stood around admiring the hole. Ladders were put in place, and Gayle descended into the ground. Finds came quickly—shovels made from ox shoulder blades, antler picks, and flint implements. All were recorded with my camera as soon as they arrived on the surface. They were then boxed and shipped

to the Society headquarters for closer examination. When Gayle came

across a large pile of animal skulls close to an area of charring on the floor

of the uncovered shaft, a chill descended over the assembled company.

I repaired with the farmworkers to

the inn while Gayle and his

associates went off to their

headquarters to identify

the bones and

other artifacts.

Embroidered Bag
Containing pieces of
mussel and oyster shells

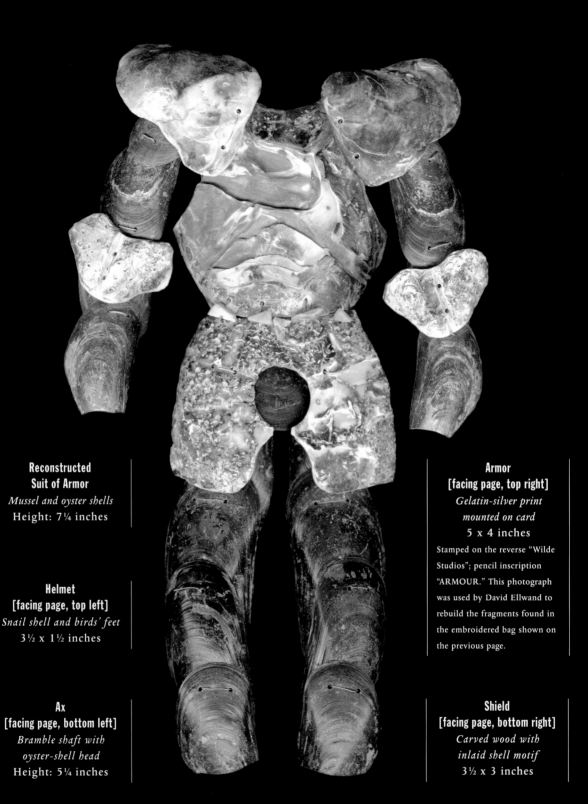

**Reconstructed
Suit of Armor**
Mussel and oyster shells
Height: 7 ¼ inches

**Helmet
[facing page, top left]**
Snail shell and birds' feet
3 ½ x 1 ½ inches

**Ax
[facing page, bottom left]**
*Bramble shaft with
oyster-shell head*
Height: 5 ¼ inches

**Armor
[facing page, top right]**
*Gelatin-silver print
mounted on card*
5 x 4 inches
Stamped on the reverse "Wilde
Studios"; pencil inscription
"ARMOUR." This photograph
was used by David Ellwand to
rebuild the fragments found in
the embroidered bag shown on
the previous page.

**Shield
[facing page, bottom right]**
*Carved wood with
inlaid shell motif*
3 ½ x 3 inches

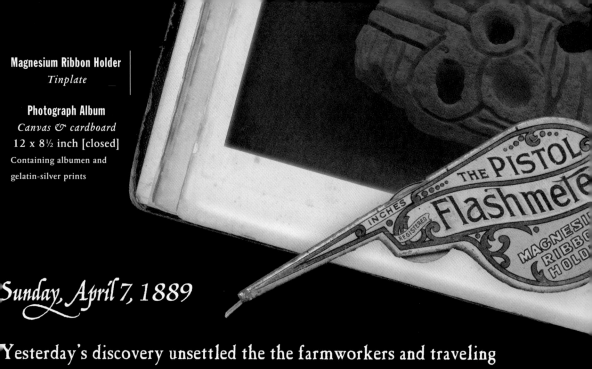

Magnesium Ribbon Holder
Tinplate

Photograph Album
Canvas & cardboard
12 x 8½ inch [closed]
Containing albumen and
gelatin-silver prints

Sunday, April 7, 1889

Yesterday's discovery unsettled the the farmworkers and traveling

laborers, who are today on their Sabbath rest. With Gayle and his

associates due to be absent for some days, I took the opportunity to

venture alone deep into the pit. I intended to take some magnesium "flash"

photographs of the workings, such as those achieved inside the Great

Pyramids of Egypt by my colleague the famous Professor Piazzi Smyth. I

was proceeding with some care to set up my reflectors and candles at a safe

distance from the two lengths of magnesium tape I intended to ignite —

a difficult and dangerous task when working alone — when I noticed some

deeply etched marks in the soft chalk at the entrance to a second chamber

Below on the floor were several broken
lumps of chalk with similar markings. I was certain those
markings were not there yesterday when I first examined the area. I felt a
chill draft, and there was a musky scent in the air. As I ducked under my
blackout cloth and focused the image on the gridplate, a light from the
depths of the cavern suddenly caught my attention. I glanced up and saw
a dark object hovering in midair, lit by a glow behind it.

Reflexively, I released the shutter. A bright light, a puff of smoke, and the object clattered to the ground. I went over and picked it up.

It was a carved wooden face, a frightening thing. It had teeth, which looked to be made of some type of bone or antler, and pointed ears.

Two flint holed stones were placed for eyes, which went straight through the wood, forming a small mask. I had an overwhelming urge to look through the holes. I placed the mask in front of my face. There was a smell, as of charred wood. Suddenly I could see them, incredibly clearly.

Two tiny pygmies, little men, no more than 12 inches high with thin tall hats, standing in the dark corner of the chamber. They looked straight through me, as though I were invisible. I felt frightened and began to panic. Quickly, I clambered up the ladders and returned to the surface, still holding the mask.

Carved Wooden Mask
[above]
Oak, flint, & teeth
Diameter: 6 inches
Front inlaid with bovine teeth and holed flint
stones; carved diagram or map on the reverse

Gateway Stone Spectacles
[right]
With the lenses removed and two holed
stones put in their place

But I knew I would have to go back down the mine — I'd left my photographic equipment there. I asked a local lad to come with me and offered him sixpence. He agreed, and we descended. The air was still thick with the smoke from my magnesium flash tape. The lad was clearly frightened and told me to hurry. I packed my photographic apparatus into its cases, and we left the mine.

My curiosity has been aroused. I believe the pixies are trying to communicate with me. Maybe they sense a fellow artistic spirit. I brought the mask back to my lodgings and examined it closely. Why had this mask appeared? And why did it let me see the pixies? I turned the mask over in my hands. The flint stones that formed the eyes must, as the old man told me, serve as a kind of lens that makes the pixies visible. I had to make myself a pair of

spectacles, which would be far less conspicuous. I took a pair of gold-rimmed spectacles and removed the glass. I inserted two of the holed stones I found on the hill. They fitted well enough. I put on the spectacles and went out for a walk.

Immediately, my vision was full of translucent flickerings. The more I stared, the more I saw, until finally, around a clump of thornbushes close to the crown of the hill, I spied a dozen or more tiny people evidently in great distress. They seemed to be screaming, and the agony shown on their faces was quite overwhelming. Quickly I removed the spectacles, and the sight was no more .

With the aid of my stone spectacles, I can see through the false world of reason inhabited by Gayle and his like and into the hidden life of the natural world around us. I must stop the dig and amend the wrongs that Gayle has done.

**Twenty-Two
Holed Stones**
Flint
Found scattered
throughout the chest

Monday, April 15, 1889

Gayle is back, gloomier and more frenzied than ever in his chopping at the earth. He has declared that he no longer needs the help of the local laboring folk, who in any case have withdrawn their cooperation. I returned to the hill this evening once the archaeologists had left and, wearing my new

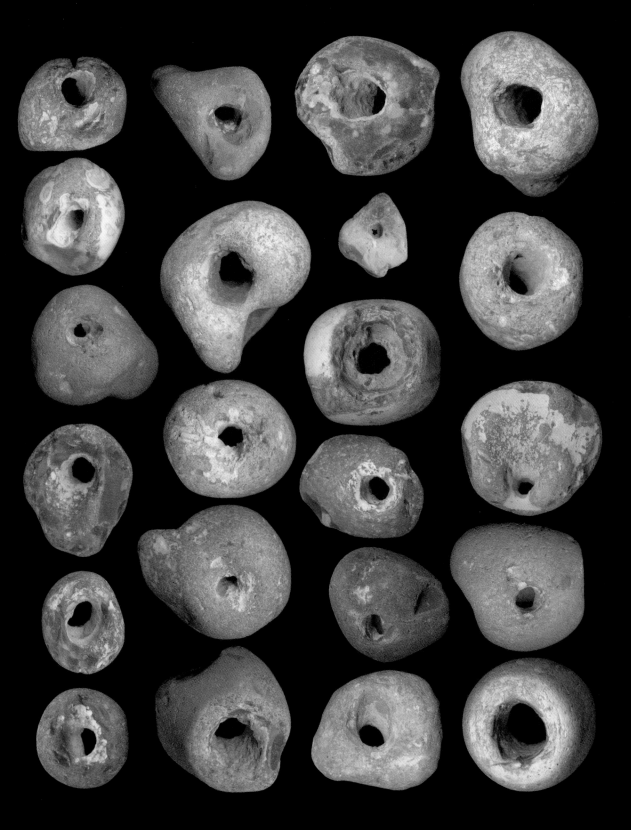

spectacles of stone, saw many figures at work, trying to repair the damage to the Settlements. Although they were silent, I could feel their anger at the cruel invasion of their home. I feel the pixies are trying to engage my help to rid the hill of Gayle and his associates. Truth be told, I feel the desire to be rid of him myself. I am determined to convince Gayle to discontinue his incursions into the ancient hillside. I shall speak to him of the Little People and of the lore that has it that any who disturb their home will be cursed. My last resort will be to get him to see them for himself. Perhaps then a shaft of humanity might penetrate the man's soul and cause him to abandon his relentless digging into the past and into the very heart of the Downs.

Wednesday, April 24, 1889

Gayle and I were alone today in the shaft when I spied a carving, similar to the last, propped up against the flint wall. Its screaming jaws seemed to be pleading for my help.

I called Gayle. "This," I said, "is a mask such as I have described to you.

Through this you may look into the other world of this hillside. Perhaps then you will come to understand the folly of your ways and leave these people in peace."

"Nonsense, Wilde! What makes you think that an archaeologist such as myself, a man qualified and experienced in the discipline, should be taken in by your shoddy workmanship? You go to laughable lengths to convince

me of your stories. I cannot understand why first a splinter becomes for you a tiny sword and now, this crude mask! Are you mad, or just a halfwitted fool? You must know that I am aware of the potential disgrace you were facing when we first met. We both know

Mask: Carte de Visite
Gold-toned albumen
print mounted on card
2½ x 4 inches

that it is not in your interest to lose the only gainful employment you have

had in a long while." He went on in such a vein for quite some time, then

finally let out a cackle of derision and tossed the mask to one side.

He is an arrogant man, and his words were chosen to injure. I picked

up the mask and asked, "Are you sure about this, sir?" He grabbed it

from me and, like a buffoon, held it in front of his face and started to

parade, skipping as he fancied the Little People might. In that moment,

I knew that I would never be able to reach him and would have to find

other means to cause him to leave the hill.

Gayle entertains his fellow archaeologists at the inn this evening with stories of my eccentricity, but it has occurred to me that here I have found a sure way of making my own fortune. For if I can see the pixies through my stone spectacles, I must be able to photograph them in a similar fashion. No such images have ever been obtained, and the photographer who achieves such a feat will be the toast of all society.

Journal Pages
Two distressed gelatin-silver prints, pasted down

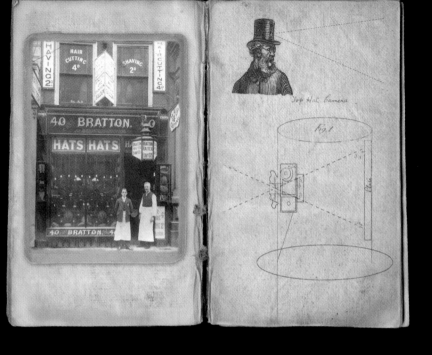

Journal Pages

*Sketches by Isaac Wilde
showing his plan for
the hat camera, and a
gelatin-silver print of
Bratton's hat shop*

Thursday, April 25, 1889

Today being my free day, I visited my friend

Bratton, the hatter, and purchased from him a rather

unusual collapsible French top hat. I brought the hat

back to the farm, made a small hole in the front, and

attached a holed stone to the exterior.

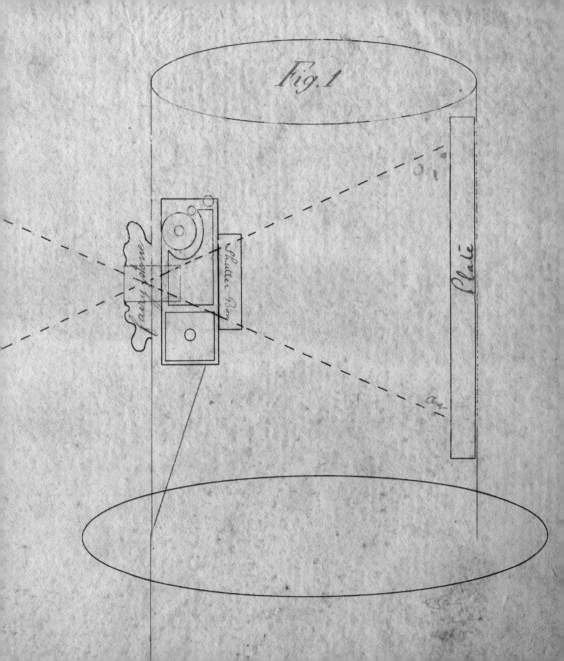

Fig.1

Fairy lantern

Shutter Box

Plate

b_1

a_1

Taking a small brass lens,

I mounted a shutter inside the

hat and attached a photographic

plateholder to the back. I took the hat into my darkroom and carefully

inserted a glass plate. Holding the rim of the hat, I pulled it down hard

over my head, sealing out all light. I left the darkroom, walked over to my

mirror, and released the shutter. I was surprised at how good the result

was when later that evening I

processed the plate.

**Self Portrait of Isaac Wilde
Wearing His Hat Camera
[left]**
*Gelatin-silver print mounted
on card
6½ x 4½ inches*

**Lens used for
hat camera
[above]**
*Brass
with wheel
aperture*

The next morning I tried out the hat camera again, and after a little trial and error I acquired more adequate results. My tests completed, I decided to visit the mine with my new equipment. Again I loaded the hat camera, put it on my head, and set out. The weather was miserable, and when I arrived at the entrance to the mine I was surprised to see the archaeologist had abandoned work for the day and had secured the entrance with some wooden planks. I removed my stone spectacles from my pocket and put them on. I looked around. It was deadly quiet — there was only the noise of the rain on my hat — had the pixies gone? I turned round slowly, looking very carefully through the apertures in the stones, and then I spied him — a pixie standing in front of the boarded-up entrance as if on guard, holding a tiny ax. I crouched down in the mud. He seemed to be unaware of my presence. Quickly, I moved forward and released the shutter. I had done it — I had captured an image of a pixie! The next few nights were spent in the darkroom, working on the negatives until I was able to make the first print.

Pixie
Gelatin-silver print
mounted on card
4¼ x 2¼ inches
Inscribed "Pixie,
copyright I. Wilde"
on the reverse

Tuesday, April 30, 1889

This evening I attended a meeting of the Photographic Society along

with Gibson Gayle; in my pocket I concealed the print I had made of

the pixie. I decided to show it to the whole group, as there could be no

better time than at a general meeting, where as well as old members,

new nominees would be present.

On arriving at the hall, Henry the chairman introduced me to a

charming young man called Arthur who quizzed me greatly about my work on the dig and in particular if I knew anything of the folklore attached to the area. I couldn't resist showing him my most recent image. I took it out of my pocket and passed it to him. He took one look and began howling with laughter. Soon, my small photograph had been handed to every member in turn, and I quickly became a laughingstock. Gayle shouted out, "How could a medal-winning photographer produce such a terrible fake?"

Later, after the formal business of the meeting was finished, I seized my chance to present the entire story to the membership, but the ridicule continued. Finally, a man from the back of the hall shouted, "If these Little People exist, capture them on a daguerreotype plate!" The room went silent. Everyone there knew that it was impossible to fake a daguerreotype, it being a one-off photograph produced straight onto a metal plate without the need of a negative. I had no choice and willingly accepted the challenge.

I returned home with Gayle, the silence occasionally broken by his laughter. He will laugh on the other side of his face when this is over.

Wednesday, May 1, 1889

I had not produced a daguerreotype for twenty-five years, so I consulted an old book of mine—H. H. Snelling's "Art of Photography," which gave me a full account of the process. I borrowed the entire apparatus—camera, lens, fuming boxes, and polished plates—from an old boy at the society. Now all I needed were the chemicals mercury and iodine. My landlady had some iodine crystals, and a trip to Bratton's procured a bottle of mercury.

Friday, May 31, 1889

It had taken me several weeks to perfect the process, but finally I had some good sharp images, one of the King Oak, a self-portrait, and a close-up of my hand. I was ready. I took the daguerrotype camera to the mine and descended into the chamber.

DAGUERREOTYPE:
A photographic process invented by the French artist Louis Daguerre in 1839. A daguerreotype is a positive-only process allowing no reproduction of the image. Therefore it is a "one of a kind" picture with no "negative" original. The process: the image is formed directly onto a copper plate that has been silvered and polished to a mirror finish. Before exposure, the plate is exposed to iodine vapor in a light-tight fuming box; this makes the silver surface light sensitive. The plate is then loaded into a camera and the exposure made. The image is developed by exposing the plate to the vapors of mercury in another fuming box. The plate is then fixed in common salt and then dried.

Amulets
Two clay figures
Approximately 2 inches high
Origin unknown

The King Oak
[previous page]
Sixth-plate daguerreotype
in a velvet-lined
gutta-percha case
3 ¼ x 3 ¾ inches closed

Isaac Wilde's Hand
[previous page]
Sixth-plate daguerreotype
in a velvet-lined
gutta-percha case
3 ¼ x 3 ¾ inches closed

Unidentified Object
*Carved wooden handle with
a brass cage attached*
7 ½ inches long

Portrait of Isaac Wilde
*Sixth-plate daguerreotype
in a velvet-lined
gutta-percha case*
3 ¼ x 3 ¾ inches closed

The atmosphere was different—cold and dank and most unwelcoming. I slipped the stone spectacles on and looked around, but there was nothing. Had the pixies left?

The Vanisher
*Gelatin-silver print
mounted on card*
5½ x 7¼ inches
Stamped "Wilde Studios" and inscribed
"The Vanisher" in pencil on the reverse

Then Gayle came in and disturbed me at my secret project. He told me I was a disgrace to the good name of photography, and he wished me well on my new career as a pauper. I now hated this man and would do anything to see him gone.

No sooner had the thought passed through my mind when there was a flicker of light and an object clattered to the floor of the mine. It was circular and appeared to be made of two pieces—a base, inlaid with bone and flint, and a flat circle on top with a crystalline pointer. A hole had been bored right through the center of both pieces and fitted with a holed stone. Gayle snatched up the thing before I could reach it. Examining it closely, he twisted the center dial around. The smile on his face was lit by the beam of sunlight that broke through from the shaft above and struck him full in the eyes. In a flash, he was gone. There was a dull thud as the instrument hit the ground and was split asunder. Before my very eyes, Gibson Gayle had vanished.

I knelt down and picked up the strange object. It was very curious. I walked around the chamber and shouted Gayle's name, but he had gone.

I slipped on my spectacles and looked round. I saw a faint light and walked towards it. Then I saw the most extraordinary thing — two pixies stood guarding something. I moved slowly towards them. They were motionless. I peered over them to see what they were protecting and saw a tiny sleeping pixie, no more than two inches long. The two guards vaporized before my eyes. Turning into wisps, they flew out of the mine. I set up the old camera and took one plate of the infant pixie sleeping before the wisps returned. I took the spectacles off, packed away my camera, put the instrument that had made Gayle vanish under my coat, and left the mine for good. Gayle's colleagues were sitting around the edge of the dig. I waved to them and returned to my lodgings.

Saturday, June 1, 1889

Early this morning, the police knocked on my door. Constable Grimshaw told me the dig has been canceled and asked me if I knew the whereabouts of Gibson Gayle. I told him that the last time I had seen him, he had been in the shaft. Grimshaw said no one had seen him since yesterday and people were getting worried that he had been lost in the mines. I replied that he had seemed perfectly well when I had left him. Grimshaw looked round the room. The vanisher was on the table. He didn't even take a second look. He told me again that the dig was canceled and went on his way.

Sleep will not come to me. Gayle's final smile flickers constantly before my closed eyelids. The vanisher reproaches me with its presence. Could it be that the Little People who made this are indeed vengeful creatures? Has the scientist gone for good?

Lodgings
*Gelatin-silver print
mounted on card*
5 x 3 inches

Sunday, June 2, 1889

I worked against time last night to process the precious image I have captured. I must leave this place before I am arrested. I have assembled my photographs and diaries and the many objects I have accumulated over the last few months — the evidence of my story — and packed them in my traveling box. I have left instructions that I will send for my box when I have secured a forwarding address. Once the fuss over the disappearance of Gayle has died down, I shall return to reclaim the image, which I am sure will prove once and for all to the doubting world the existence of the pixies.

In order that none may repeat Gayle's tragic experience, I have split the two halves of the vanisher and buried one half in an old tin hatbox. I alone shall be able to locate it on my return to the hill.

Daguerreotype
Unmounted
6 x 4½ inches

Mr Wilde's top hat
[following page]
5 x 7 inches
Stamped "Wilde Studios" on the reverse

I finish now in haste.

I must seal the box.

There is a knocking at the door.

PART THREE

Being the final part of David Ellwand's journal

So that was the story of Isaac Wilde.

I would have dismissed it all as complete nonsense had I not seen the mysterious light through my own stone—and, yes, of course I've tried wearing Isaac's stone glasses, but they show me nothing; they just make me look ridiculous.

On my desk is the top of the vanisher. I think it's made of oak, well polished, with what look like bone pieces inlaid. I have discovered the most curious thing— if I spin it around, the crystal always returns to the same place; moreover, to my astonishment, if I leave the crystal pointing in another direction, it will always slowly, over several hours, return to the same place, like some weird compass.

It may seem obvious, but it took me an age to figure out that the crystal wanted to lead me somewhere, and of course I had to follow. I thought the best place to start had to be the woods. I packed a camera, minidisc recorder, and the piece of the vanisher into a bag and set off.

Previous page:
Will-o'-the-Wisp

Vanisher Dial - *Carved oak inlayed with bone, flint,*
and lead with a crystal pointer 5 inches in diameter

When I reached the wood, I placed the piece of the vanisher on the ground. I walked around it a few times, then stood looking at the view through the trees, my back resting against an old oak. Suddenly, I was frozen to the spot, unable to move. There was a rush of cold air and a strange, musky scent. My heart fell to my boots. I heard a groaning sound in the trees below and called out, "Is anybody there?" Silence. I looked quickly around through the copse. Nothing. I returned to the vanisher, and it had rotated to a different position. I picked it up and walked in the direction the crystal pointed. Just as I started to walk, I saw a light in the distance, darting through the trees like a low-flying comet blazing its trail. Immediately, I put my camera to my eye and pressed the shutter. I didn't believe there'd be anything on the film, the light was so bad, so I put the camera away and looked at the glowing ball. It hovered for a while and then disappeared. This was all too much for me. I felt scared. I had no option but to leave the woods and return home.

Will-o'-the-Wisp

When I developed the picture that night, the photo was out of focus but the glowing wisp was there. A chill went down my spine as I compared the picture I had taken with the pictures Isaac had taken more than a century before.

Main image: Will-o'-the-Wisp

Inset image: Ghostly Orb - Toned albumen print mounted on card; stamped "Wilde Studios" and inscribed "Ghostly orb" in ink on the reverse

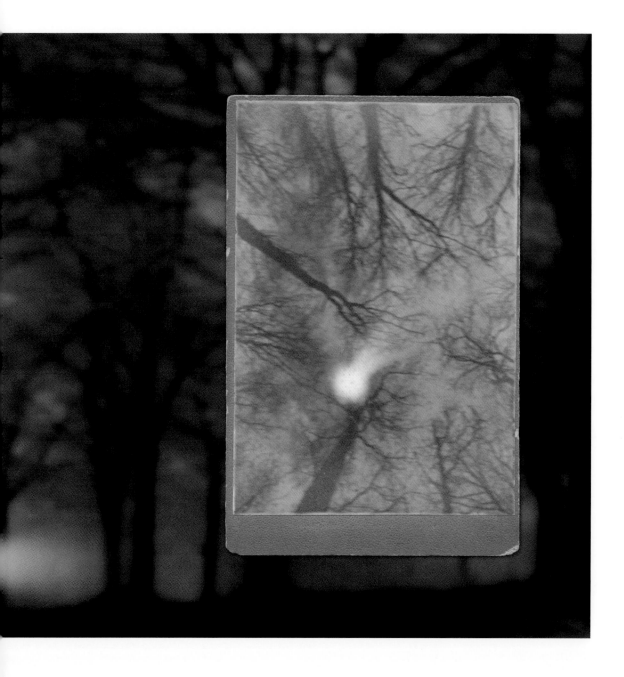

I told no one about what had happened. Who would believe me? It took me several days to pluck up the courage to return to the Downs, but eventually I did. Again, I followed the pointer, and this time I was led into the deepest, darkest woods I'd ever seen. I held my nerve and just kept following the pointer until eventually the thing pointed back on itself. I placed the strange wooden object on the ground, and it started to spin. This was the place! I picked up the pointer and examined the ground it had been sitting on. I rummaged around in the grass and moss and uncovered a flat stone. I kicked at it, and the moss fell off, revealing an etched spiral. This definitely was the place. I lifted the stone and started to dig.

The earth was hard, filled with rocks and bits of flint. I broke the surface, then went down on my hands and knees and started scraping. Before long, my nails grated against something metallic. I dug around it, clearing more and more earth. All the time, I was taking photographs, snapshots, really, as a record of what I was seeing. Finally I pulled the container out of the ground. There it was—Isaac's hatbox, in almost perfect condition, protected by a smeared layer of sticky grease. I sat back and took some pictures before putting the camera down.

Marker Stone with Spiral Carving ⁄
Kodachrome transparency

Following Page: The Dig ⁄ *Marked 35-mm contact sheet*

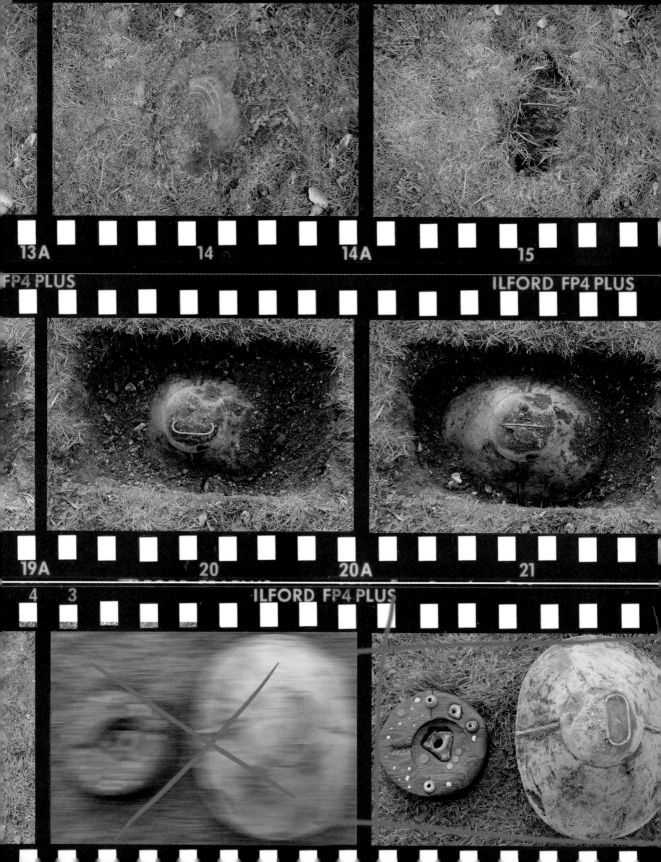

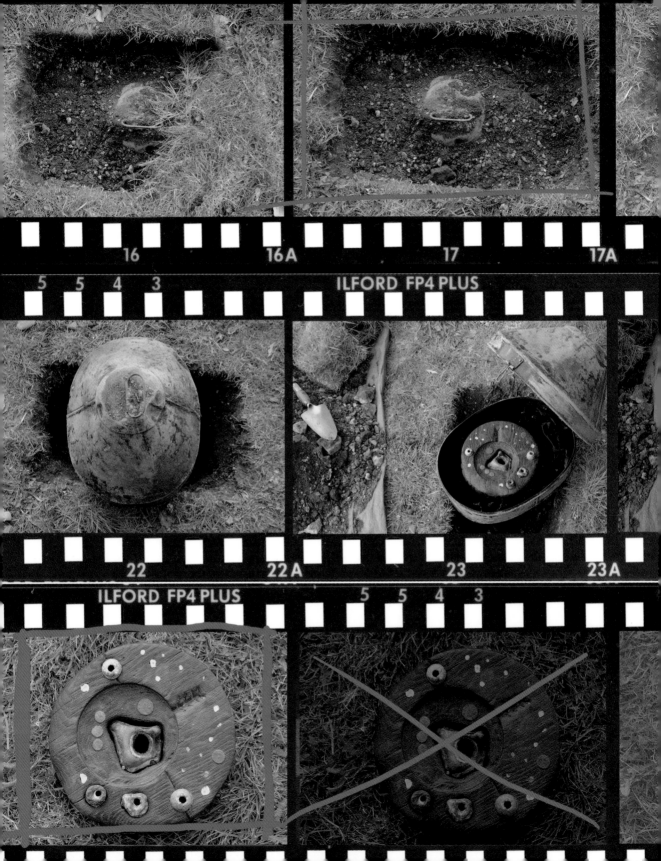

ILFORD FP4 PLUS

The lid was tight, but gradually I pried it open. Here was the missing link! Inside the tin, the other half of the vanisher rested on a piece of black velvet, just as Isaac had left it. A faded powdery perfume escaped from the velvet nest, along with the scent of charred wood. I took the heavy wooden disk out of the tin and examined it more closely.

Just as I was about to retrieve the top half of the vanisher from my bag, I felt a cold draft, and then I heard a swishing. I might have imagined it, but there also seemed to be laughter coming from deep in the woods below, the laughter of an old man. As I stared into the gloom, I realized it was getting quite dark. I felt I was being watched, and my mind conjured up a shadowy figure standing among the tree trunks. Forcing myself to stay calm, I repacked the tin. I carefully refilled the hole, replaced the earth, and trod it down with my boot. And quickly got out of the place.

It wasn't until I got back home that I realized there was something else in the hatbox as well. Under the velvet was a small, highly ornate daguerreotype case.

At sunrise the next morning . . .

The Base of the Vanisher and the Hatbox

I dropped the centerpiece into the base and slowly turned the pointer.

Once you've looked through the vanisher, it's never the same.

Poppy Field Leading to Barrow Hill ⁄

Kodachrome transparency

"King of the Pixies"

Sixth-plate daguerreotype in a velvet-lined
gutta-percha case

3 ¾ x 3 ¼ inches [closed]

Discovered by David Ellwand in the base of Isaac Wilde's hatbox

Photograph by Isaac Wilde
Looped Tree
Gold-toned albumen print
5 x 7 inches

Text copyright © 2008 by David and Ruth Ellwand   Photographs copyright © 2008 by David Ellwand

First U.S. edition 2008

Library of Congress Cataloging-in-Publication Data is available.

Library of Congress Catalog Card Number pending

ISBN 978-0-7636-2096-7

2 4 6 8 10 9 7 5 3 1

Printed in China

This book was typeset in Poliphilus, Blado Italic, Caslon Antique, Ludovico Woodcut, Franklin Gothic, and Columbus. The photographs were created with magic and necromancy.

Candlewick Press, 2067 Massachusetts Avenue, Cambridge, Massachusetts 02140

visit us at www.candlewick.com